COFFEE WITH

GROUCHO

C O F F E E   W I T H

GROUCHO

SIMON LOUVISH

FOREWORD BY FRANK FERRANTE

DUNCAN BAIRD PUBLISHERS

LONDON

Coffee with Groucho
Simon Louvish

Distributed in the USA and Canada by
Sterling Publishing Co., Inc.
387 Park Avenue South
New York, NY 10016-8810

This edition first published in the UK and USA in 2007 by
Duncan Baird Publishers Ltd
Sixth Floor, Castle House
75–76 Wells Street, London W1T 3QH

Managing Editors: Gill Paul and Peggy Vance
Co-ordinating Editors: Daphne Razazan and James Hodgson
Editor: Jack Tresidder
Assistant Editor: Kirty Topiwala
Managing Designer: Clare Thorpe

Library of Congress Cataloging-in-Publication Data Available
ISBN-10: 1-84483-515-4   ISBN-13: 978-1-84483-515-7
10 9 8 7 6 5 4 3 2 1
Printed in China

Publisher's note:
The interviews in this book are purely fictional, while having a solid basis in biographical
fact. They take place between a fictionalized Groucho Marx and an imaginary interviewer.
This literary work has not been approved or endorsed by Groucho Marx's estate.

CONTENTS

Foreword by FRANK FERRANTE

When I was nine years old I saw the Marx Brothers in *A Day at the Races* and my life changed. Exhilarated and empowered by the antics of Groucho, Harpo, and Chico, I began the first of many pilgrimages to my local library where I began to unearth all things Marx.

In 1976 my father drove me to the Ambassador Hotel in Los Angeles from our tiny suburb of Sierra Madre so I could catch a glimpse of my hero—my hero from *Duck Soup*. ("I can see you in the kitchen bending over a hot stove. But I can't see the stove.")

Shuffling to the podium, 85 year-old Groucho Marx arrived, sporting his trademark beret. He mumbled responses to audience members. And then the question was posed, "Groucho, are you making any new Marx Brothers movies?" The pause was deafening. "No," Groucho retorted, "I'm answering stupid questions." The audience erupted. It was Groucho at his grouchiest. It was glorious. And it was beyond imagination that ten years later I would be portraying Groucho from age 15 to 85 in the off-Broadway production of *Groucho: A Life in Revue*, written by his son Arthur.

When interviewed about the many years I've spent portraying Groucho Marx, I'm often asked the same question, "Why Groucho?" Is it his irreverence? His disdain for all things conventional? His shark-like verbal assaults? His word play? His outrageous appearance—the rectangular greasepaint mustache, the dancing eyebrows, the ubiquitous stogie, the mussed hair and darting lope?

Yes to all that. But there is considerably more at the core of what makes Groucho and his comedy still appeal to me and countless millions. Groucho Marx, the man and the comedy persona, is the voice of the disenfranchised. The voice of the little guy, the outsider. Groucho is the kid who stands tall and fearless and lets us know that the emperor has no clothes. He is a truth teller. His comedy pulverizes the privileged, the wealthy and powerful. And Groucho skewers those who often control our fate—politicians, professors, doctors, and lawyers. (She: "You're awfully shy for a lawyer." He: "You bet I'm shy. I'm a shyster lawyer.")

Groucho Marx is an alter ego for all of us hapless souls taught to play by the rules unconditionally. At nine and under the thumb of a particularly stern teacher, I needed Groucho Marx. I needed to *be* Groucho. I needed to rise and intervene on behalf of my petrified classmates and raise hell, crack wise, and give that teacher the treatment Groucho reserved for longtime foil Margaret Dumont in *A Day at the Races*.

Several years ago, after a performance in Easton, Pennsylvania, I was approached by a man my age. He grinned and said, "You're the guy. We all wanted to be Groucho and you're the guy who got to do it."

Today I share Groucho's legacy by giving performances in New York, London, Toronto, and even the towns the Marx Brothers themselves played while on the vaudeville circuit—Altoona, Dubuque, Paducah. In one audience, there's a 94 year-old woman who saw the Marx Brothers on tour in 1928. She's laughing. In another, there's a six year-old boy who's never heard of Groucho. He's laughing.

Yes, my hero, the laughing will never stop. And our "Secret Word" to you is "thanks."

INTRODUCTION

At the height of his career, Groucho Marx was said to be the funniest man in the world. For nearly half of the 20th century, from the 1920s to the 1960s, he was a dominant figure in American comedy. First as one quarter of the Four Marx Brothers, then as one third, and then on his own, he developed a unique style of sardonic quipping on stage, then on screen, and then on television's early cathode ray tube.

Groucho's image became as familiar in his age as Charlie Chaplin's had been for the first generation of movie fans: the slick master of wisecracks with a painted mustache and jiggling eyebrows perched over drooping spectacles, cigar clutched in his fingers as he loped toward the latest butt of his attacks on the sacred cows of society. But as a working actor Groucho always knew that a joke was only as funny as an audience would allow it to be. Drawing people into the Marxian universe of creative lunacy had depended in the first place on combining his own talents with those of others. To have people rolling in the aisles, there had to be the small matter of an act.

That act was the family unit of the Marx Brothers—Groucho with Chico, Harpo, and Gummo on the stage, and when Gummo left, with the youngest brother, Zeppo. Together, they endured a long, familiar apprenticeship in vaudeville halls, before conquering Broadway in 1924. From 1929, they made thirteen movies together before bowing out as a team. But of the brothers, it was Groucho who survived into a new stardom on television, in his hit show, *You Bet Your Life*.

Like the best of comedians, Groucho's humor was based not just on a carefully honed technique, but also on his family background and the historical period in which he grew up—on the experiences of a generation of Americans who were new immigrants, or the sons and daughters of immigrants, who came seeking new opportunities in what they saw as a promised land. These early comedians presented themselves as court jesters to a seething republic that was rising to a new prosperity, and which would soon face the crisis known in the 1930s as the Great Depression. In this crisis, it was the Marx Brothers'—and Groucho's—task to quip their way out of trouble, to comment on the panic and madness around them, to cast their jokes like thunderbolts at all and sundry, break all the rules, leap over the boundaries, and confound all received wisdoms.

Groucho died 30 years ago, in 1977. It is the conceit of this book to revive him, for one night only, at one of the favorite haunts of his old age, for a post-

mortem nosh and some light and imaginary prattle
about his amazing life and his times. Groucho, of
course, had his own inimitable take on everything:
"The secret of life is honesty and fair dealing. If you
can fake that, you've got it made."

GROUCHO MARX (1890–1977)
His Life in Short

Julius Henry Marx, alias Groucho, was born in New York City on October 2, 1890. His German-Jewish parents, Samuel and Minnie Marx, had separately emigrated to America, Minnie from northern Germany in 1879 and Sam from Alsace soon after. They had married in 1885, losing a first son in infancy. Groucho's older brothers, Leo and Adolph (alias Chico and Harpo), had been born in 1887 and 1888. He was to have two younger brothers, Milton (Gummo), born 1892, and Herbert (Zeppo), born 1901.

Groucho's mother had been a touring performer in Germany with her parents, Lev Schoenberg (a magician) and Fanny (a harpist) before her family emigrated to New York. There, on the Lower East Side,

the Schoenbergs had to settle for a life of hardship—
and Fanny put her harp aside until it was noticed by
her grandson Adolph, who took to it instantly and,
as Harpo, became a player of real quality.

Groucho's childhood was spent much further
up the East Side, in Yorkville, a more middle-class,
mostly German neighborhood. His father Sam
was a reasonably accomplished tailor, despite the
many tales his boys would later tell of his ill-fitting
pants. While Sam worked, cooked family meals, and
played pinochle with his peers, Minnie tried to keep
the kids in school and out of trouble. She was not
keen at first that any of them should go into show
business, remembering her harsh life on the road.
But she worried about the early gambling habits of
her eldest and favorite son (Chico), and to redirect
his energies she bought a second-hand piano. Soon
he was playing in dance halls and at the early movie

nickelodeons. Meanwhile, Harpo took to playing the piano, too, among many odd jobs, famously plying his trade at Mrs. Alma Schang's "Happy Times" brothel in Long Island, in 1907.

By this time, young Groucho, who was determined to compete with his brothers for Minnie's attention, had already become something of a veteran performer. A keen reader of adventure stories, he could sing well, and was the only one of Minnie's sons who actively wanted to follow in the footsteps of a family mentor, his uncle Al Shean. This was the stage name of Minnie's younger brother, who had become a successful vaudevillian, with an act called the Manhattan Comedy Four, singing Irish and German songs. His later partnership with an Irish performer, Ed Gallagher, became one of vaudeville's most long-lived acts as "Gallagher and Shean." The pair were immortalized decades later in Neil Simon's play and then movie, *The Sunshine Boys*. Al Shean adopted a nasal German-Jewish comedy accent that became a prototype for many followers, and was shamelessly imitated by Groucho when, as Julius Marx, he first went on stage by himself, aged 15, in 1905.

Taking his fate in his own hands, Groucho had answered a classified ad in the *New York Morning World* calling for a boy singer for $4 a week with room and board. The act was called The Leroy Trio, and Groucho, having auditioned by singing "Love Me and the World is Mine," got the job alongside Mr. Leroy and an East Side dancing kid called Johnny Morris. Leaving home with a shoebox containing some pumpernickel bread, bananas, and hard-boiled eggs, he commenced his life-long showbiz career.

Groucho's first appearance on stage was in drag, as Mr. Leroy's specialty was female impersonation, but the job was cut short when Leroy and Johnny Morris eloped together and stranded their third partner in Cripple Creek, Colorado. Groucho returned to New York, pretty saddle-sore but now a fully-fledged actor. At this point, Minnie decided to take over his bookings, and secured him a job with an English actress, Lily Seville. Miss Seville appeared with her new partner in Dallas on Christmas Eve, 1905, in an act called "The Lady and the Tiger." The *Dallas Morning News* reported that "Miss Seville is a typical Yorkshire lass … Master Marx is a boy tenor, who introduces bits of Jewish character from the East Side of New York."

The inevitable fate of small-time vaudeville acts intervened, however, as Lily Seville ran away with the tiger tamer, and Groucho returned again to New York. This time Minnie got him a job with a solid outfit, "Gus Edwards' School Boys and Girls." This provided the prototype for an act which the Marx Brothers would soon develop for themselves. When, on April 18, 1906, the city of San Francisco was hit by earthquake and fires, the Gus Edwards' performers appeared at a Metropolitan Opera benefit, on May 3, and Groucho sang "Somebody's Sweetheart I Want to Be" to a capacity audience of 3,000 people.

The following year, Minnie enrolled Groucho and Milton (Gummo) in Ned Wayburn's summer School of Vaudeville in 1907, alongside little Fred and Adele Astaire, and a girl singer, Mabel O'Donnell, who joined the two brothers as "Wayburn's Nightingales." This gave Minnie her first chance to manage her offspring herself, as she independently opened "The Three Nightingales" in Coney Island in November 1907. Soon, Minnie got rid of Mabel O'Donnell and replaced her with a nice Jewish boy, Lou Levy. But she was still desperate to rescue her eldest sons,

Chico and Harpo, from a life in low dives and seedy Bowery halls. By June 1908, Harpo had joined the act, which became "The Four Nightingales"—Harpo's debut as a singer! This gave the brothers their first major tour of fleapits around the nation, with Minnie and her sister Hannah even joining the act at one point. At the same time, Chico was touring as an "Italian" pianist in various double acts. In 1910, the family had relocated from New York to Chicago, the hub of the Midwest's vaudeville circuits. And in 1911 the four brothers finally teamed up, presenting their extended sketch, *Fun in Hi Skool*.

The Marx Brothers' school act, which was relaunched as *Mister Green's Reception* and then revamped again under the title *Home Again*, lasted in its various forms for over eight years. At some time in this period, the brothers acquired the backstage nicknames of Groucho, Chico, Harpo, and Gummo while still appearing on stage under their given names of Julius, Leo, Adolph, and Milton. In one legend, a fellow performer called Art Fisher came up with the names that would immortalize them during a card game. There was a vogue at the time for nicknames ending in "o." Groucho was probably so named for his grouchy character, rather than, as some suggest, for the "grouch-bag" that vaudevillians carried their money in. Chico famously chased "chicks," Gummo wore rubber-soled dancing boots, and Harpo had discovered his grandmother's harp and had begun playing his own. He had also, by this time, found that he could never remember his lines on stage, and decided to be a mute. Only after 1922 did the Marx Brothers finally transfer their nicknames to their comedy careers.

Between 1911 and 1919, the Marx Brothers crisscrossed America, playing vaudeville halls large and small with Minnie as their manager, and Sam tagging along. Chico had suggested they each adopt a different ethnic character, to identify with the diverse immigrant audiences. He already had his Italian act. Harpo played an Irish character before shutting up, and Gummo was the straight man. Groucho was the teacher or father figure, continuing at first with Al Shean's German-Jewish accent. But in May 1915, while war raged in Europe, the American liner *Lusitania* was sunk by a German submarine, and all German acts became suspect. Overnight, Groucho changed his voice to his own purely Yankee twang.

During the war, Minnie Marx was highly agitated at the thought of split loyalties, with her American identity at odds with her German cultural roots. Her solution was to keep her sons out of the army by reconfiguring them as working "farmers" exempt from the draft. The Marx Brothers' incompetence as farmers, however, soon brought them back to the stage. In the event, only Gummo enlisted, in October 1918, just as the war was ending, and he thereby left the act for good. In his place, the youngest brother, 17-year-old Herbert (Zeppo), was drafted to keep the act as "The Four Marx Brothers."

By 1919, Groucho had already developed the character that was to stand him in good stead for the rest of his life—the worldly-wise, unflappable ad-libber, never at a loss for a word or a put-down. The act, however, was getting a little tired, and Al Shean's gags were pretty long in the tooth. Postwar America was a new world, at the start of a new decade which would become known as the "Jazz Age." The brothers needed new writers, Groucho more than the others, as his humor was essentially verbal. A fellow vaudevillian, Herman Timberg, provided a script for a musical show, *On the Balcony*, in 1921. By now,

Groucho was married, to a dancer, Ruth Johnson, and in July 1921 their first son, Arthur, was born. Legend recounts that Groucho was so distracted that he rushed from his wife's hospital bed to the show without having time to paste on his mustache properly, and so he daubed on a stroke of greasepaint instead. And this is how the Groucho we know got his finishing touch.

In 1924, the Marx Brothers had their first runaway Broadway success with *I'll Say She Is*, written and composed by the brothers Will and Tom Johnstone. This madcap revue transferred from Philadelphia to Broadway, where it ran on into 1925, and brought them to the attention of the New York élite. In 1925, *The Cocoanuts* opened with a script by ace playwright George S. Kaufman and songs by Irving Berlin. The show also featured a key future collaborator: comedienne Margaret Dumont, who would be a fixture in the Marx Brothers' movies, playing society ladies. In 1928, Kaufman, with co-writer Morrie Ryskind, wrote them a second show, *Animal Crackers*, which became an even bigger hit. Audiences came back night after night, as the brothers kept varying their act, adding new gags and situations.

By this time, motion pictures had finally learned to speak, and sing. Around 1920, the brothers had allegedly made a short silent movie, *Humorisk*, but, owing to confusion in a projection booth, it vanished after its first and only screening. Now, however, the time of the verbal comics had come, and in 1929 Paramount Pictures produced the first Marx Brothers movie, a direct adaptation of their stage hit, *The Cocoanuts*. This was followed in 1930 by a version of *Animal Crackers*, and from then on the Marx Brothers were movie stars.

Monkey Business, *Horse Feathers*, and *Duck Soup* followed in quick succession, establishing the Marxes as the sound movies' pre-eminent comedy team of brothers. Inevitably their lives changed as their fame grew. For over twenty years, they had spent almost every day together, as a team on the stage. Now they spent much of their lives apart. By this time, Groucho had two children with his wife Ruth—Miriam, their daughter, having been born in 1927. The marriage itself would eventually become rocky, though it rattled through the next batch of movies, made for MGM: *A Night at the Opera*, *A Day at the Races*, and the less successful *Room Service*, *At the Circus*, and *Go West*. By *The Big Store*, in 1941, the Marx Brothers seemed to be getting stale. Groucho's marriage ended in divorce soon after, in 1942.

For Groucho, in particular, fame and wealth did not end feelings of anxiety that traditionally dogged vaudeville performers, ever fearful of a downturn in audience affection. Comics, more than others, dreaded the moment when the well of inspiration dried up and the laughing stopped. Hollywood may have provided an illusion of security, with its sun-soaked hills, beautiful villas, and swimming pools, but for this son of immigrants Sam and Minnie Marx, nothing was certain. Only the wisecracks could endure. Minnie had died in 1929, and Sam in 1933. The other brothers had children of their own. And Hollywood kept throwing up new talent to ring the box office tills. The era of mid-1930s censorship had curtailed the brief period of out-and-out Hollywood comic anarchy that had empowered W.C. Fields, Mae West, and the Marx Brothers.

By the 1940s, World War II found the Marx Brothers tired, and they made no movies together after 1941 until *A Night in Casablanca*, five years later.

In July 1945, Groucho married Kay Gorcey, and his third child, Melinda, was born in 1946. The following year, Groucho began a new career, presenting *You Bet Your Life*, a quiz show that lasted three years on radio and eleven further years on TV. By the time of the TV show the greasepaint mustache had been replaced by a genuine, gray one. The celebrated patter had slowed, and adjusted itself to the stricter code of television, but the show's popularity revived Groucho's fortunes and maintained his fame through to the 1960s.

The Marx Brothers' last joint movie was *Love Happy*, in 1950, a most *un*happy project starring Harpo, with Groucho and Chico in subordinate roles. Groucho made guest appearances in several movies and starred in three: *Copacabana* in 1947, co-starring fruity Carmen Miranda; *Double Dynamite* in 1951, with Jane Russell and Frank Sinatra; and *A Girl in*

Every Port in 1952, with William Bendix. But without his brothers to match his wisecracks, all three failed to strike sparks. While both Chico and Harpo sought TV shows of their own, only Groucho's perennial *You Bet Your Life* kept the Marxian flag bravely flying.

Groucho's marriage to Kay ended in acrimonious divorce in 1950, and in 1954 he married Eden Hartford, a Beverly Hills model he had met on the set of *A Girl in Every Port*. This marriage lasted for fifteen years, but ended badly as well, with Eden citing Groucho's "uncontrollable temper" and "hostile and abusive moods." In 1971, aged 81, Groucho became romantically involved with Erin Fleming, a young woman he had employed as his assistant. This was to lead to bad blood among his family, as claims and counter-claims about her influence were made in the twilight of his years. Chico had died in 1961, and Harpo in 1964, devastating the surviving brothers.

Gummo would die four months before Groucho, in April 1977, but Groucho was too ill to be told. He faded away in August of that year, and only Zeppo remained, as an echo, until 1979.

In 1959, Groucho had published his autobiography, *Groucho and Me*, his third book since *Beds* in 1930, which had been followed by *Many Happy Returns* in 1942. Another book of comic essays, *Memoirs of a Mangy Lover*, would be added in 1963, and a compilation, *The Groucho Letters*, in 1967. Of all his work, Groucho was most proud of his writings, which were held to be the equal of the great comic literary talents of his day, such as S.J. Perelman and Robert Benchley. Many short pieces had appeared from the 1920s in *The New Yorker* and other journals.

After Julius Henry Marx had disappeared under the greasepaint, two Groucho Marxes remained. The more familiar one cavorts on the screen, fixed by the camera in moments of time that express a totally free spirit, a voice untrammeled by convention, casting doubt on hallowed truths that may well be delusions, redrawing reality in distorting mirrors, and subjecting the language itself to a mangling which leaves it panting for air on the ropes. But there was another Groucho Marx, one who desperately desired a kind of social acceptance, a place in the card games of those clever writers who met at the Algonquin Hotel in New York and who shaped a liberal skepticism in 1920s America. Their opinions, criticisms, and writings battled conservatism and promoted social changes that were at least partly achieved by Roosevelt's 1930s reforms.

Groucho's was a voice that, behind the jokes, never forgot the immigrants who crowded onto boats in Europe, with Lev Schoenberg and Samuel Marx, to make a new life in the "Goldeneh Medineh"—the

Golden Country. We can see this in *A Night at the Opera*, when the brothers stow away from Italy to New York, or in *Monkey Business*, when they are discovered in another ship's cargo hold, hiding inside barrels, but boldly singing "Sweet Adeline."

NOW LET'S START TALKING …

Over the following pages, Groucho Marx engages in an imaginary conversation (set in his favorite deli, Nate 'N' Al's in Beverly Hills), in which he responds freely to searching questions. The conversation covers twelve themes.

The questions are in red italic type;
Groucho's answers are in black type.

GETTING STARTED

Life among New York's immigrants at the turn
of the 20th century was raucous and chaotic. In
their crowded apartment at 179 East 93rd Street,
the five sons of Samuel and Minnie Marx had
to compete for attention with each other, and
with their mother's extended family. Minnie
managed her sons' lives from the start. Her
brother, Al Shean, was already a vaudeville name
by the end of the 19th century. He provided
the template for the unique brand of Marxian
humor, and wrote the original early acts that the
young Marx Brothers performed on the stage.

Groucho Marx, it's a pleasure being with you here at Nate 'N' Al's, your favorite deli.

Well, either I'm dead or my watch has stopped. How long have I been gone? More than 30 years! At least the clientele are now younger than I am. Harpo used to steal spoons here you know.

We'll get to that later. But seeing as we're celebrating your life and your movies, I thought I'd start at the beginning.

I don't remember that, I was only a little baby.

That was Chico's joke, wasn't it—from Duck Soup, *if I remember correctly?*

Well, all's fair in love and war. And dry cleaning. Say,

can you take this tux and bring it back Friday? It was a little close in the coffin.

Well, you were all a little close, weren't you—the five brothers?

We had to be close. My parents only had two beds, and they slept in the big one. It was tough in New York in those days. My mother loved children—she would have given anything if I'd been one. Say, were there only five of us? That apartment was pretty crowded. My mother had five sisters and two brothers, and my father had a whole bunch who said they were relatives, but I think they just liked playing pinochle. He could never remember where he was exactly. Once when he went on a train to join us on tour, he had to phone my mother and ask her, "Minnie, where am I?"

So it was your mother who organized everything.

She invented the Marx Bothers. Before that we were
Ned Wayburn's Nightingales. That was just me and
Gummo and this girl called Mabel O'Donnell. Where
is she now, I wonder? Probably right over there, with
the kasha varnishkes. Have you ever tried to eat a
plate of kasha varnishkes here? You have to stand in
the plate and eat your way out. Boy, they don't stint
on the portions.

*Your first act was a solo, in 1905 I believe. You were 15,
and you did "Impersonations of the Yiddischer."*

Believe me, those were no impersonations. All that
stuff came from my Uncle Al. He had the Manhattan
Comedy Four. They sang Irish songs in all the joints
in the Bowery. Then he did Jewish sketches. *Quo*

Vadis Upside Down and *Kidding the Captain*. You know, the Captain says, "Now listen, a lady here has lost a jeweled garter." "A Jewish garter?" "I'll give you the measurements—it's the size of a calf." "That's almost a cow!" "I'm giving you the right steer!" "I hope you're not handing me a lot of bull." Well, they laughed at that in 1902.

Didn't he write for your first acts?

I had nothing but confidence in him, and very little at that. I began with his material, then worked my own lines in. Harpo couldn't remember his lines, so in the end he stopped talking and became a mute. Had this German comic type fright wig—big red thing. Of course, in the movies you didn't see the color.

What about Chico and Gummo?

Chico had the Italian act. He got it from his barber. It was his idea we should be different types like that. The Jews would like the Jewish stuff, the Italians would laugh at Chico, and the kids would laugh at Harpo. Gummo was the straight man. He had a speech impediment, you know, he used to stutter. So we made him sing. He didn't like that, so he left. That was during World War I. I was doing Uncle Al's German-type dialogue. But after a U-Boat sank the *Lusitania*, audiences didn't think Germans were so comical. All the German acts had to become Dutch acts. I was Mister Green. Harpo would come in and say, "I'm Patsy Brannigan, the garbage man," and I would say, "Sorry, we don't need any." Chico would come up and say, "I would a-like to say goombye to-a your wife," and I would say, "Who wouldn't?"

ADAPTING TO WAR AND THE MOVIES

When America entered World War I in 1917,
Minnie Marx was desperate for her sons to avoid
fighting against her mother country, Germany.
To prevent this, she put them to work as farmers
for a while, but soon let them loose again to
hone their humor. When they began making
pictures Groucho was quick to see the difference
between constantly adapting jokes on the stage
and working to more or less fixed scripts in
movies. While admiring the skills of the various
writers who produced screenplays for the Marx
Brothers' movies, he still found ways to adapt
the dialogue and the gags.

Your mother, who was managing your show, kept you out of the army during the war.

They didn't want us at the front. We were too busy with arrears.

But she got you a job as chicken farmers, in Chicago.

We laid eggs for the war effort. The chickens were supposed to do it, but the rats ate their eggs. So we had to buy some to stick under 'em. Ours were the only chickens that laid eggs ready with the seal of good housekeeping. The seal was in another act. We kept him on, as our barker. That wasn't very good, was it?

Not really.

Well, all the jokes can't be good! Say, you haven't

stopped talking since we got here. You must've been vaccinated with a phonograph needle. Don't you have any good questions? Have we met somewhere before? I never forget a face, but in your case I'll make an exception. What do you think they've done with our pastrami sandwiches? They're the best in the country, you know. At least you can fit them in your mouth. At the Carnegie, you have to hire somebody to jack your mouth up to get the pastrami in. Here's a good question: What stands on two legs, sings in the winter, and it never rains but it pours?

I give up.

You see! *(pleased, flourishes cigar)* That was the whole idea of those dialogues with Chico. We just went on till the joke was all cleaned up. Remember "Why a duck?"

Why a duck?

Exactly. Why a-no chicken? Then we would go on till there was nowhere else to go. We would do that on the stage until the gag was played out, then carry it just a little bit further. You asked me about the movies …

No, I haven't yet.

But you're getting to it! You're getting to it! You can't fool me, I know your little tricks! I never liked watching the movies. Because there was nothing you could change. On the stage, you could change everything. Some lines made the audience laugh, other lines just died. So we would adjust things all the time. That's why *The Cocoanuts* and *Animal Crackers* ran for years on Broadway. People kept coming back because it was different every night.

But for some of your pictures you still had the chance to test out the dialogue in vaudeville-type tours, on the road. Didn't you do that when you made A Night at the Opera?

That was Irving Thalberg's idea. Our producer at MGM. He was a genius, but he died young. He was the only producer we dealt with who was worth his salt. He let us go out on tour and we tested different scenes. Like the stateroom scene, when we're all there together and the crew all pile in: "And make that two more hard boiled eggs!" That was written by Al Boasberg. He used to write sight gags for Buster Keaton. Then he worked for Milton Berle. He was great. George Kaufman, Morrie Ryskind, Bert Kalmar, Harry Ruby. They were great writers. They knew our stuff and wrote into our routines. We did our best work with those guys.

And S.J. Perelman.

S.J. who???

He wrote Monkey Business.

Him and who else? Listen, I wrote him his best review once: "From the moment I picked up your book until I laid it down, I was convulsed with laughter. Someday I intend reading it."

There were some great gags and lines in that movie.

A lot of that was from our previous stuff. All that sketch about imitating Maurice Chevalier? That was from *On the Balcony*. And we did that kind of material before, in other acts. When Chico says, "My father was a-partners with Columbus," and I say, "Columbus has been dead for 400 years!" and he says, "Well, they *told* me it was my father."

Your grandfather was a bit closer to Columbus, wasn't he? Lev Schoenberg, the Prussian magician. That was around 1850.

Well, they *told* me he was my grandfather. I knew him as the umbrella man. He tried to make umbrellas. And to teach me and my brothers our reading for our bar mitzvahs. But I could never remember the lines. He just sat in the house and mumbled. My grandmother, she was the one with the harp. She brought it all the way from the Old Country, so she said. It took Harpo some time to get around to it. But once he started, he never left that harp.

FAMILY, MARRIAGE, AND CONSEQUENCES

Family, to the Marx Brothers, became a different story when they grew up and started to marry. Groucho's first marriage, to Ruth Johnson, produced two children, Arthur and Miriam. His second and third marriages did not endear him to the battlefield of divorce and alimony, American style. Trying to mix the joys of home life with the traveling life of vaudeville was always difficult, but once in Hollywood there were other pressures. To Groucho, there were pros and cons in fatherhood. Even small daughters might rebel when coaxed to follow father into show business.

You teamed up with your brothers for more than twenty years, on the stage. Four of you, then a fifth, when Zeppo joined. Day in and day out, sleeping in the same rooms, rehearsing and playing together. That's unusual for siblings, to be so close.

We worked ourselves up from nothing to a state of extreme poverty. It's cheaper if you're together. But I guess you're right, we were always close. That's what worked for us on the stage and in the movies. Because each one of us knew what the other was thinking. And if we dressed up like each other, it was hard to tell us apart. That's how we could do the scene in *Duck Soup* where Harpo breaks a mirror and covers up by playing my reflection in the empty frame when I come along. Harpo and Chico were even closer in looks. Zeppo used to dress up like me, too. But he didn't like being a follower. Because he

was always the baby, the youngest. So after *Duck Soup*
he called it a day. We were down to three—Harpo,
Chico, and me.

And by then, you had families of your own. You married
your first wife, Ruth Johnson, in 1920.

She got her looks from her father. He was a plastic
surgeon. Well, you know what they say: love goes out
the door when marriage comes innuendo. We had
some good years. When my kids were born. We were
still on the stage then. When we got to Hollywood,
we tried to be members of the Country Club, but
in those days it was restricted. You know what that
meant? No Jews. Everybody wanted in because they
had a great swimming pool. So I asked them, Can
my son get in the water up to his waist? He's only
half Jewish.

What about your other wives?—you married three times.

I guess I thought I'd get better at it. As they say,
you're only as old as the woman you feel. Our coffee's
here. Shall we raise a toast? Here's to our wives and
our girlfriends—may they never meet. You know
in America we love to divorce. Who was it who said,
"The husband who wants a happy marriage should
learn to keep his mouth shut and his check book
open?" Was it me? Well, whadayaknow. But marriage
simply kept getting more expensive. Paying alimony
is like feeding hay to a dead horse. That was one of
mine, too. I'm being pretty witty tonight. I should
come back to this place more often.

*But in the end, you quite enjoyed being a home-loving
kind of guy. Weren't you interviewed on TV by Ed
Murrow in your garden?*

That was when I was trying to grow my own avocados. I planted an avocado tree, but nothing happened. Then somebody told me I had to have a male and a female tree. Can you believe it? So I planted them, but they just stood there, didn't even look at each other. I still wonder what an avocado tastes like. But I did love my little orchard. It's the sap in me, I guess.

After you've moved through a thousand lousy boarding houses you'd like to put your feet up, too, I'll bet. It was a crazy life, on the road. One place in the early days the floor was so thick with roaches, we had to put tin cans full of water down and place the bedposts in 'em. Another time one manager paid us in pennies, and we had to cart our wages off in sacks.

After Ruth you married Kay Gorcey, and you had a third child, Melinda.

She was real cute. As was my wife. She was a gay divorcee. Not gay the way the word is used nowadays. They first started to use that in the sixties. What was it they talked about then? Prophylactic sexuality? Or was it polymorphous? I was never good with big words. I did read that sort of stuff once in a while. Freud, Jung—he was about as Jung as I was, the old goat!—and Krafft-Ebing. Boy was my craft ebbing! We moved into Sunset Plaza Drive about then. Kay knitted socks for the baby. We got a Chinese chef to cook us dinner. I read a lot of books and played happy families.

And then there was Eden, your third wife?

I met her on a movie set. *A Girl in Every Port*. That was with William Bendix. Well, I couldn't take William Bendix home, could I? It was Eden for a while. Sooner or later, I guess, things became too normal. So then we broke it up. After the third marriage, I guess I decided to call it a day.

Your first two kids, Arthur and Miriam, didn't go into show business. But didn't Melinda appear with you sometimes, on TV?

That was on *You Bet Your Life*. Years later she told me she never liked performing. But when you're eight years old, what else can you do? When I was eight I was imitating Uncle Al. "Vas has gesachta? A fair gemacha, vot ve got from de vidow Rosenbaum ..." Or was that Joe Welch? He was an Irishman, you know, with a Jewish act. Everything was jumbled up in those days.

STAGE vs. SCREEN

The Marx Brothers' first two movies were direct
versions of their most successful stage plays,
The Cocoanuts and *Animal Crackers*. These two
plays had led the transformation of Broadway
in the 1920s from a more conventional style
of stage comedy to a wilder approach, more in
tune with the "Jazz Age." Both in the plays and in
their Hollywood adaptations, The Marx Brothers
began to be defined not only by their own antics
but by their collaborators: the comedienne,
Margaret Dumont, and the writers—George
Kaufman, Morrie Ryskind, and others—who
helped round out such immortal characters as
Captain Spaulding.

Let's get back, or forward, to Hollywood. I'm not sure which way we're going.

Keep it up, keep it up, you're doing fine. I have a pretty good shrink lives next door who can straighten you out in no time and empty your pockets in a minute. If you go off in a huff he can do it in a minute and a huff. That was a good one, wasn't it? Ask away.

Your first picture was The Cocoanuts, *which was a straight version of the stage revue that had opened in 1925. How did you find working in the movies?*

It was easy, we just took the streetcar. That movie was shot at the Astoria studios in Long Island. Soon after we made it, they closed down the studio. I guess we were too much for them. *The Cocoanuts* had been a big hit on Broadway. We ran for 377 performances before we went on the road. George Kaufman wrote the book and Irving Berlin did the songs. "The Monkey Doodle Doo"—did you know that Irving Berlin wrote that? No wonder he became famous. Why didn't I think of that?

It was a play about the Florida land grab …

That was a real crazy time in America. People got suckered into buying lots on land that was only fit for alligators. This was before the Wall Street Crash and everybody believed in something for nothing. I had some good lines in that, if I can remember. "Do you know that property values have increased 1924 since 1,000 per cent?" "Do you know that this is the greatest development since Sophie Tucker?" … and so on. But who remembers Sophie Tucker nowadays. She was a great lady, but they tore her down and built a department store where she stood. That was a joke we used on Maggie Dumont. She was in that show, every night, taking our gags. I don't know how she survived.

You used to say that she never understood your jokes, all those years. But it turns out she was trained as a comedienne, long before she came with you on the stage.

That must have been in the Roman period. She left the stage before World War I to marry a millionaire, but he died. So it was moider, you see. She tried to be a society lady. But she had to go back and wear greasepaint and schmutters on the stage. We gave her a real hard time, particularly Harpo, who kept climbing on her and chasing her all over the stage. Of course, he chased every skirt.

Nowadays if you do that on or off the stage, they clap you in jail on a harassment charge.

Why didn't *The Times* tell me that? It gets awfully lonely in the cemetery, so I keep up my subscription.

When you were kids, you also had a cousin, Pauline, in the house. Was she a prototype Maggie Dumont for you, a kind of elder sister that you drove crazy? Maybe you were reliving your childhood.

Did we ever leave it? This is the territory of Doctor Freud again. Me, I was just a ham actor, and he was the big cheese. But we can't get into that stuff, surely? I thought this was a family book.

Okay, so back to the movies. You didn't answer my first question.

Was that the question of the first part? Or the question of the second part? Now you're making me feel dizzy.

The question of the first part …

I never liked that part. Let's get on to the second part. No, sorry, we already did that. Let's take it all from the top. The point is, the movies paid much better. When you've grown up in show business, you talk about the money all the time. By the time we got to the movies, we were rather long in the tooth. I was nearly 40 years old, Chico was 42, and Harpo was 937. He came to us in a consignment of old Aztec urns. We had to shake him for three days to make him squeak. That was about as far as we got. You know we made a silent movie of our own once, back in 1920. I was the villain and Harpo was something else in a top hat, sliding down a coal chute. We shot it in a day and then previewed it in some fleapit in the Bronx. There was a bunch of crazy kids in the audience who kept climbing over the seats and running in the aisles. It was like a Bowery matinee. Nobody paid any attention to our movie. We were so flustered, we left the film in the theater, and when we went to screen it to Alex Woollcott and George Kaufman and company, it turned out the reel in the can was our negative. So we left that in the projection booth, too. That was our career in silent movies. But in the talkies, we were a hit.

After The Cocoanuts, *you filmed* Animal Crackers, *your second movie.*

That's right. The second movie always comes after the first. If you go on like this, kid, you might graduate. *Animal Crackers* was also written by George Kaufman, and he brought in Morrie Ryskind. He was a great gag writer. He could get into our heads and write the stuff as if we'd made it all up ourselves. But I was the one who came up with Captain Spaulding. He was a real character, an old fire-eating vaudeville act. They called him "The Man Who Was Hotter Than Vesuvius." Imagine that, eating ashes for 25 years—I didn't do that till I was married.

"My name is Captain Spaulding, the African Explorer— did someone call me shnorrer?—hooray hooray hooray."

Bert Kalmar and Harry Ruby wrote that. Great song writers. That was my best act with Maggie Dumont. She was Mrs. Rittenhouse, the society lady. There was a line in that song that the censor cut out of the movie. She says, "He is the only white man who covered every acre," and I say, "I think I'll try and make her." They snipped that out. But we got away with Morrie Ryskind's line, "One day I shot an elephant in my pajamas, how he got in my pajamas I'll never know." He was a great radical socialist when he was writing for us. You can tell, can't you? Later on he supported Richard Nixon. He got so right wing he fell off the scale.

POLITICS AND THE DEPRESSION

Despite the comedy, Groucho always had
strong political opinions, supporting left-wing
causes during the 1930s. Those were the years
of the Depression, of the Civil War in Spain
(1936—1939), and of the coming to power of
the Nazis in Germany. Groucho's opinions
were not unusual, as many Hollywood actors
and directors had radical and left-wing views at
that time. After World War II, these sympathies
became suspect as the Cold War with the Soviet
Union began. The "witch-hunt" of Hollywood
subversives gathered force, but Groucho,
curiously, was never called on to testify before
the House Un-American Activities Committee.

Let's talk politics. It turns out that the FBI kept files on you from the 1930s. You supported various left-wing causes: trade union rights, the anti-fascist forces in the Spanish Civil War, and Russian War Relief in World War II.

Well, the Russians were on our side then. Or were we on theirs? I only know that when the Nazis invaded them, the Russkies put a sign on their door saying, "Help Wanted." Harpo wasn't available so I gave them a broom to clean out a machine gun nest. They sent it back with a nice note, too, but all the bristles were shot off.

The Daily Worker wrote in the 1930s that you were a person of impeccable working class origin. That was in the FBI files, too. J. Edgar Hoover was keeping a close eye on you even then.

So that was who was sneaking around my room!
I thought it was Greta Garbo! Oh me oh my! I don't
know about working class. I always go first class if
I can. Well, politics makes strange bedfellows, but
then so does marriage. Everybody in Hollywood
was on the left in those days. Except W.C. Fields. He
always liked to be contrary. We were all rooting for
Roosevelt—he went Republican. But we were all
scared by the Depression. People were living in huts
in the cities, and breadlines stretched all over Los
Angeles. The country was going to the dogs and even
millionaires were jumping out of windows. Maybe
they looked like windows of opportunity, but I doubt it.

And then Harpo went to Moscow, in 1933.

That was Alex Woollcott's idea. He was the *New York
Times*' critic. He loved Harpo—but he had his Marxes

all mixed up. Everybody knew Harpo didn't speak, so he couldn't make an ass of himself out there. We were all pretty innocent in those days. I would have gone to Moscow but I had a mustache and only Stalin was allowed to have a mustache in Russia. We weren't crazy about Russia anyway. Maybe Harpo thought he could chase some of those Russian blondes. What we all believed in was FDR and the New Deal and getting the country back to work, and fighting for democracy. So when the Nazis took over in Germany, we had to make a stand against Adolf Hitler. When Harpo went through Germany to Russia, he saw all the brownshirts out in the streets in Berlin painting signs saying *Jude*—"Jew"—on Jewish shops. And then, when the war came, we all had to do our bit. The government wanted to win the war, so they left us out of the army. We went all around the country telling jokes to the soldiers. They were pretty grisly jokes but the troops didn't mind. You could crack an egg and they'd find it funny. Those were not happy days. I had dinner at the White House once, but they didn't even serve pumpernickel.

But then, after the war, all those old alliances with left-wing causes started to be investigated.

Right. We had Senator Joe McCarthy. He saw Reds everywhere—in the government, in the army, in the toilets of the Waldorf-Astoria, and in Hollywood. Boy did he see red in Hollywood! He was nuttier than a fruitcake.

Before that, in 1947, lots of Hollywood liberals and radicals got called to testify to the House Un-American Activities Committee. Ten Hollywood writers and directors went to jail for refusing to testify. But you were

never called before the Committee. They let you alone.
Why was that, do you think?

Of course I was called. But I was called Archibald.
So I never answered. What were you called in those
days?

I don't remember. I was only a little baby.

Touché. And three-ché. Well, that wraps up politics.
Aren't we having a great time here? You should try
the blueberry custard. They don't serve it here but
you should try it anyway.

I think you were never called because the Committee was
afraid of your jokes.

It's very kind of you to say so, sah.

Thank you.

No, thank you.

No, thank you.

No, thank you. How long is this going to go on? I have a dental appointment at three o'clock, and believe me, it has to be less painful than this.

THE MARX BROTHERS IN HOLLYWOOD

The Marx Brothers reached Hollywood in a new golden age for American screen comedy, the era of the talking clowns. New Yorkers born and bred, they had to adapt to the more leisurely pace of Los Angeles, like so many other actors hit by the Wall Street Crash and the closure of Broadway theaters. Comedians had to find a way to renew their old stage routines and jokes to appeal to a nation-wide audience. Groucho called this pleasing "the barber in Peru"— meaning Peru, Illinois. The jokes changed and so did the Marx Brothers' comic style.

Let's get back to the movies.

And about time, too. I was about to look for the exit.

After the two movies shot on the East Coast, you made Monkey Business *in Hollywood, in 1932. The uncredited producer on that picture was Herman Mankiewicz, who is best known today as the scriptwriter of* Citizen Kane.

Well, we didn't see much of him. We had a great director, Norman McLeod. He was a real gent and let us do what we wanted. He used to say about himself, "I'm as quiet as a mouse pissing on blotting paper."

Your writers on Monkey Business *were S.J. Perelman, Will Johnstone, and Arthur Sheekman. How did you work with the writers?*

Sheekman became a great friend. We had a whole lot of laughs together. Perelman had a bunch of fancy ideas. But I told him our jokes had to work with audiences all over the country, not just in New York. When you're a writer you can just sit down with your thoughts and make yourself laugh in the mirror. It's great fun and I love to do it. But in show business, if the audience out there doesn't laugh you're off to the employment office. George Kaufman used to say we taught him something. He used to think if the audience wasn't getting one of his lines in New York City, he could keep it in the script because it would go down better in Boston. But we taught him he had to change the gag. We liked to use our old material best, stuff that had been tried and worked on the stage. The good writers understood this. They had to work out of our own characters. Then we would be okay.

So Monkey Business *had a lot of material from your old stage plays, like* On the Balcony, *and even that old* Home Again *sketch. A lot of the stuff on the ship.*

Exactly. But there was some new dialogue. When I say to Chico, "Does your grandfather's beard have any money?" And he says, "Sure, it fell hair to a fortune," I don't think we used that before. We did use a lot of gags that we worked into our radio show, *Flywheel, Shyster, and Flywheel,* recorded in those years. Most of them were never used in the movies, though. Like when Chico, who's my detective assistant, comes in and I say to him, "What have you been doing all week?" And he says, "I've been chasing ice wagons." And I say, "I thought I sent you out to chase ambulances." And he says, "Sure, but ambulances go too fast." All that stuff's lost now.

You know, somebody did find those scripts and published them.

They did? And I didn't get my cut? This is outrageous! Call for my attorney! *(stands on seat)* Is there an attorney in the house? *(thirty people stand up in the café)* How're you doing, folks? Nice weather we're having today.

(Helping Groucho down from his seat) *But you didn't use the detective, Wolf Flywheel, until* The Big Store, *in 1941.*

Well, I was the slow one of the family. I had to work out all the angles. Phew, I'm not as spry as I used to be. I used to dance on tables all night. It was always a gala day. And a gal a day was enough for me, I can tell you. Those were the good times.

When you first moved out to Hollywood, it was a very different life from New York, wasn't it?

It sure was. I made ten times more money. We went first to a place called the Garden of Allah that was very swanky but had too many noisy parties. Then we moved out, my wife Ruth, the two kids, and me, to a rented house in Beverly Hills. After that we found a place of our own on Sunset Plaza Drive. That was like paradise. And all our friends were coming in from New York anyway. Broadway was still in trouble and everybody was in the movies. Harpo fell in with the big shots as usual. His friends took him up to the Hearst Castle. He always got on with everybody. George Bernard Shaw was there, too, you know. Harpo had met him in France. They both liked nude sunbathing. I was too shy for that.

Your next movie was Horse Feathers. *You were Professor Quincy Adams Wagstaff, of Huxley College. That had some schoolroom scenes that must have been straight out of the old* Fun in Hi Skool, *your very first Marx Brothers sketch.*

Yes, they were pretty similar. "And now we find ourselves among the Alps. The Alps are a very simple people who live on rice and old shoes. But the Lord alps those who alp themselves." Then Harpo and Chico would shoot peas at my back. That was a great show. I think it was our biggest hit. We got on the cover of *Time* magazine. Zeppo was my son in that one. And, hey, I did get to dance on the table!

That's my favorite Marx Brothers moment. Your song, "I don't care what you have to say …"

"… it makes no difference anyway—whatever it is,
I'm against it! And no matter how you change it or
condense it—I'm against it!"

That seems to have been your motto.

Well, those are my principles. If you don't like them,
I have others.

DUCK SOUP, PACIFISM, AND THE RULES OF COMEDY

In 1933, after *Monkey Business* and *Horse Feathers*, the Marx Brothers made *Duck Soup*, which many consider their greatest and funniest movie. The Depression, and lingering memories of the terrible human price of World War I, made social satire and pacifism popular, and *Duck Soup* remains comedy's great anti-war statement. As with many of their movies, early drafts of the script contained an even sharper satire. The Marx Brothers' pictures demonstrate how screen comedy is constructed, how all comedy stems from character, and how the plot and gags follow from that general rule.

For most of your fans, Duck Soup is still their favorite
Marx Brothers movie. But it's different from any of
the others, I'm sure you'd agree. It has an anti-war
message that was very relevant to a later generation,
who rediscovered it in the 1960s.

Yes, they loved it, all those crazy kids with long hair
and beads. They said it was much funnier if you
smoked marijuana in the theater. But I never wanted
to be a member of a club that would have me as a
member, so I stuck to ordinary cigars.

In the movie, you were President Rufus T. Firefly of
Freedonia, a fictional European state that was being
bankrolled by Mrs. Teasdale, played by Maggie Dumont.
Chico and Harpo were your spies against the rival
country of Sylvania, and Zeppo was your secretary.
The director was Leo McCarey.

He was great. He really knew about comedy timing. Other directors we had just directed the traffic on the set. But he was an expert. He'd worked for Hal Roach, the king of slapstick, for years. You know Hal put Laurel and Hardy together? They were always coming apart. They were like two big babies. At least we were grown up. Except Harpo. We got him in a garage sale at the orphanage.

It was the only movie in which Harpo and Chico didn't play the harp and the piano.

We all thought that would slow down the action. Their music acts were great but you needed to give them time on the screen. You know, of course, those two aren't really acting when they play those scenes. They're just being themselves. Harpo needed to concentrate when he plucked that harp, and Chico played the piano practically from the cradle. But *Duck Soup* was another kind of comedy. If you slowed down the action, you'd lose the thread.

It was also very much a political satire, wasn't it? The best comment on war is when the Sylvanian ambassador Trentino tries to talk you out of starting one and you say, "It's too late, I've already paid a month's rent on the battlefield." Can you talk a little bit about how you chose that subject?

Well, in those days people remembered World War I and how countries had blundered into it because their leaders didn't want to stand down. It was a pointless argument and millions of people had been killed. We sent hundreds of thousands of Americans out there and got back a whole load of coffins. It was called the "war to end all wars," but in the 1920s we had books and stage plays like *The Big Parade*, which became a great movie, showing what a waste it all was. Then again, in the Depression people were getting fed up with politicians and governments. There was a crazy slogan, before Roosevelt: "Prosperity is just around the corner." But you turned the corner and it was just the same cheesy mess as before.

The first script written for Duck Soup *was called, for some reason, "Cracked Ice." And in that version, you and Chico and Harpo were gun runners. You were an armaments merchant and they were trying to sell you ammunition and cannons. Why was that cut out? Did the studio think it made your character too nasty?*

There were so many versions of scripts, I can't remember. We had armies of girls typing out new scripts every day. The writers teamed up in twos and worked in different offices, and they passed these scripts between them. Then I would usually take 'em and make sure the scenes would work for us. The rule of comedy is, everything comes from the characters. The plot follows from the characters, and that provides the reason for the gags. But some scenes can just stand on their own. Like Harpo's fight with a lemonade vendor that ends up with him paddling in the lemonade with his dirty feet. That was the kind of sight gag we always needed for Harpo. Chico and me were just about part of the real world, but Harpo was on another planet. He was all libido and we were all ego. Boy, were we ego. I'm not so ego these days, particularly for this interview.

The best sight gag in Duck Soup *is the mirror scene. Were you aware that that was a gag from a Max Linder silent movie?*

Sir, are you accusing me of chicanery? Of course, you know this means war! There used to be a vaudeville theater in Chicago where the manager posted a list of jokes that were so corny they should never be used again on that stage. So everybody copied them down and used them in the next town. There were joke books, like Madison's *Budget*, and McNally's *Bulletin*, and everybody subscribed and took what they wanted from them. The best way not to get stale is to use the gags that fit your character and stay away from the rest.

But the mirror gag was exemplary. You can see in that movie how close you are as brothers, because a small change of make-up makes all three of you look the same.

When Chico and Harpo were younger they'd stand in for each other and nobody noticed. The main point of

the characters is that they were both idiots, and I had
to deal with all the crazy things they came up with.
This was stuff we'd been doing on the stage from
1911. You have to admit that's a pretty good score.

DOCUMENTARY TRUTH, FICTION, AND COMEDY

The Marx Brothers always thought they were making pure comedy, and had no other aim but to make the audience laugh. But since their comedy was so unique and personal, it couldn't fail to contain many allusions to their own early life as the sons of immigrant parents. *A Night at the Opera* has often been seen as a fond memory of the passage from Europe to America viewed through the Marx Brothers' distorting lens. The brothers' comedy was subtly changed here by their new producer, MGM's Irving Thalberg, who tried to give Groucho, in particular, a softer, more "human" image.

After Duck Soup, *you had a rift with Paramount, and you began making movies for MGM. Your first MGM picture was* A Night at the Opera, *which one critic said shows that in every Marx Brothers movie there's a documentary screaming to get out.*

Well, it can scream all it wants to, that's all I have to say. After all, everything we made was fiction, which is a pack of lies.

But there's a truth in that description. After all, your parents and their family all came over to America on the kind of immigrant ship in which you all stow away in that movie.

Well, the funny thing about that was the censors didn't want us to mention anything about Italians in that movie. They said if the first part of the picture was set in Italy, that would upset Mussolini. Well, you couldn't Mussolini all of us. That line was in the script but they cut it out, can you believe it? Now we're getting into politics again. Let's get back to stories.

It's pretty clear the early scenes in A Night at the Opera *are in Milan, at La Scala. That's where you tell the horse-cab driver he should have slowed down his horses because "on account of you I nearly heard the opera." A whole scene between you and the driver was rehearsed but never made the movie.*

That's show business. We had enough writers on that one to have written *Gone with the Wind*. In fact we should have written *Gone with the Wind*—it won a pile of Oscars and made millions of bucks. All I got was spaghetti and meat balls. Anyway, Irving Thalberg

recut the movie and we were pretty happy with it.
He was our favorite producer. He was just a kid, you
know. I think he took over at MGM when he was 12
years old. Give or take ten years or so. He turned that
studio around. All L.B. Mayer had to do was lie on a
couch and have vestal virgins feed him grapes. If you
could *find* a vestal virgin anywhere in Hollywood.
Most of them took off their vests.

There was a famous story about the time you broke into
Thalberg's office and roasted chestnuts in his fireplace.

They must have been pretty old chestnuts. Or was
it weenies? He always used to keep everybody
waiting. Hollywood's biggest stars were sitting in his
waiting room. Greta Garbo, Jean Harlow, Maureen
O'Sullivan. So everybody liked sitting around there.
Jimmy Stewart, Spencer Tracy. Johnny Weissmuller

was swinging and hollering on the drapes. But you could spend the whole day and Thalberg didn't turn up. So one day we just got fed up and barged in, with our lunch. When he turned up in the end, he just started talking business, didn't turn a hair. He was a mensch.

And he suggested that you go out on tour before shooting, to test the scenes with an audience?

We went out to Salt Lake City, Seattle, Portland, and all over California. We had the writers with us, Morrie Ryskind, Al Boasberg, and our co-stars, Kitty Carlisle—great kid—and Allan Jones. He came from a long line of Welsh miners. They had to have a long line—there was no work in Wales. So they came over here. He was a good kid, and he could sing, too. He could sing and dig coal at the same time, so that kept us going through the winter. Remind me, what we were talking about? Boy, do you ever keep on the subject? That subject must be pretty lonely, trying to figure out where you've got to.

A Night at the Opera, *and was it a true story?*

It was a big hit, that's for sure. Thalberg made sure the writers wrote in all sorts of human interest. We were pretty raw before. Our idea of romance was Harpo and his horse. Thalberg made us all a bit softer. Also, we had Maggie Dumont and Sig Rumann, who always played German heavies. He was a crazy sort of guy. You know he collected insects. He would bring in snakes and spiders from the Mojave desert into the studio. At least that kept Louis B. Mayer out. We already had a snake on the set, our director, Sam Wood. Before he died he wrote in his will that nobody in his family would get a nickel unless they signed an affidavit that they had never been members of the Communist Party. And they thought *we* were crazy.

In that movie Rumann was the manager of the Metropolitan Opera and Margaret Dumont was the rich backer. It was a kind of frontal assault on the idea of high art and social snobbery.

Did you call me a shnorrer? My hearing isn't what it should be these days. People said we were against the opera but that was all wrong. The whole idea was art for all the people. Look at the stateroom scene where all the Italian immigrants and the steerage passengers mix in the party and we all hog the free food. Allan Jones sang "Così-Cosa," Chico played the piano, and Harpo did his harp act.

One of your best scenes, and there are many others.
There's the one where you insult Sig Rumann in the
restaurant, the contract scene—the party of the first part
... the scene in New York with the three bearded airmen,
the cop chasing you around the apartment but never
finding you in the same place, and the grand finale at
the Metropolitan opera, when you mess up Lassparri's
performance and all the backdrops go up and down.

Poor old Walter King, who played Lassparri, had
his kid in the audience on the set. And when the
audience starts throwing rotten fruit at Lassparri,
the poor kid gets upset and starts shouting, "They're
throwing things at my daddy!" You know, maybe it
was a documentary after all.

SURREALISM AND INSECURITY

The heady days of the talking comedians in the early 1930s didn't last very long. The renewed Hays Code of 1934 restricted what could and couldn't be said and done in movies to a greater degree than before. Financial structures also changed, reducing the power of the studio bosses. The Marx Brothers continued to make movies, but the old anarchy was not the same after they lost their greatest Hollywood champion, Irving Thalberg. Being embraced by European surrealists such as Salvador Dalí was little comfort. Despite the surreal Doctor Hackenbush, these two worlds didn't mesh at all!

*In the mid-1930s, the Marx Brothers' movies gained
another fan, the surrealist painter Salvador Dalí. He
came over from Spain in 1935, and was a big hit in New
York. Then he traveled to California and met Harpo.*

I never met him. He was the original fruitcake. He
didn't speak any English and Harpo didn't speak
Spanish or French. So they got along fine. I think
Dalí gave him a harp with strings of barbed wire, all
hung with spoons. Harpo never played it. I wonder
why? Dalí also wrote a script for us, but it was useless.
Harpo flushed it down the toilet.

*It does exist. I read it in Paris. It's pretty weird but not
funny. He didn't understand that American humor
has to be based on some kind of reality. Except Harpo's,
I suppose. But how did you feel, being fêted by the
surrealists?*

Fêted? We did the gag about a gala day already, didn't we? My God, this is the longest interview I've ever had and I haven't made a dollar on it. We didn't know anything about those people. Later on they put a bicycle wheel and a toilet bowl in the Museum of Modern Art, can you believe it? If I'd have known, I could have given them my used pants and a cuspidor from the Orpheum in Kansas City before the Wall Street Crash, and I wouldn't have had to sweat nights. Those people made all that stuff in lousy attics and now it sells for millions. Why didn't they tell me? You know I came to this country without a nickel in my pocket and now—I have a nickel in my pocket.

Well, once you got to Beverly Hills you didn't have to worry about money.

We came up from vaudeville, and in those days you

always worried about money. There was no social security, and when you fell off the bandwagon you were left in the gutter and thankful that you still had your underpants. You never forget that life on the road. That was why our mother drove us so hard. She remembered the rough life back in the Old Country. To tell you the truth, I never felt secure. I'd have sold a bicycle wheel to the museum for two cents, if I could get it. You forget a lot of things in life but you never forget poverty.

After you made your most successful pictures, up to the mid-1930s, did you feel that movie making changed at Hollywood?

Well, it wasn't the same for me at all after Thalberg died. We'd just started making *A Day at the Races*. We were two weeks into the shoot when Thalberg got ill. He just caught a cold and died. Can you believe it? The guy was 35 years old. If I'd died when I was 35 years old, only the family dog would have remembered me. But Thalberg was already famous and had made a heap of great movies. Maybe I didn't get such a raw deal out of life after all. Maybe I should quit complaining.

But after Thalberg, making movies wasn't fun any more. It was all just about making money. He had a passion for the pictures. And you know, when they made better pictures, the studios made more money. But later on the studios were just run by money people who were put in there by the banks. They didn't understand movie making.

Still, A Day at the Races *was another classic. You played Doctor Hackenbush, which was probably your best role since Captain Spaulding.*

It was supposed to be Quackenbush but some real Doctor Quackenbush came out of the underbrush and threatened to sue. Can you beat that?

The scene everyone remembers from that movie is the one with the tutsie-frutsie ice cream—when Chico sells you a set of useless books, to figure out the odds on the horses.

Chico was always giving out the tutsie-frutsie. He gambled, you know, from the time he was 12 years old. He would drive with his wife and kid and say, "I'll bet you ten bucks the lights will go green before we get to the crossing." We always had to get him out of trouble. He was going to casinos and clubs and losing money to some pretty nasty customers. Guys with sharp suits who were pissed he wasn't a real Italian. Gummo had to bail him out. After he left the stage, Gummo got into the agenting racket and had a whole stable of great actors in Hollywood. Everybody trusted him. He would go to people like Bugsy Siegel to get Chico off the hook. Later on we had to make a coupla movies just to get Chico from being dropped in the reservoir with a cement overcoat. I had a cement overcoat once but I couldn't move from the house with it. I had to go back to seersucker suits. Boy was I seersuckered.

But you made another three movies for MGM, after the one you made for RKO in 1938, Room Service, *which was adapted from a Broadway play. That was the only time the Marx Brothers played characters that had not originally been created for them.*

I was looking for another way out. You know, I was getting tired of playing Groucho all the time. I looked in the mirror and I was beginning to look like a cross between Mephistopheles and an opium peddler on the Mexican border. But *Room Service* was not so bad. Then we did *At the Circus*. That started from a story by Ben Hecht. By the time fifteen other writers got their mitts on it, it ought to have been called "A Day in the Madhouse." We just walked through that one. I had a good song, "Lydia the Tattooed Lady." "For a dime you can see Kankakee or Paree— or Washington crossing the Delaware …" We had some good scenes with Maggie Dumont and an escaped gorilla. If you could tell 'em apart. But it was just one long turkey shoot from then on. And the war had started in Europe. It was a bad time all around. I saw Reds under the bed and fifth columnists climbing through the window. I was divorcing Ruth, and pretty soon I was divorcing my brothers. I got custody of the mustache, Harpo kept the wig, and Chico bought a Buick with the alimony. Have you ever had to pay alimony?

No, never.

Well, it's always all-i-the money you've got.

THE LAST HURRAHS AND
GROUCHO ALONE

After glory comes the inevitable decline. Despite
the continuing popularity of their pictures, the
Marx Brothers were getting tired of making
movies. Old performers inevitably become
rusty, and old routines pall. Groucho was to find
a new lease of life on radio, as an early talk show
host. Shouted down by the horrors of World
War II, old-style wisecracking comedy had had
its day. But old performers just soldier on, and
even without his brothers Groucho could still
star in movies. The question was, did the old
star still twinkle, or was it time to hand in the
well-worn badge?

Did you know that in England, during the Blitz, Winston Churchill calmed himself down by watching one of your movies? He wrote in his memoirs about "the merry film clacking on."

I didn't know that. Well, good for him. There was a man who liked his cigars. He lived to be about 100, too. Now they tell me you can't smoke in public any more. They put you away in San Quentin. I sure hope he wasn't watching *The Big Store*.

It could have been Go West. *That had some great gags, like the scene on the train when you chop the carriages up bit by bit to feed the engine.*

All the studios were doing "Go West" pictures. Universal had made a movie with Jimmy Stewart and then one with Mae West and W.C. Fields. Talk about fish and fowl. They were about a 110 years old between them, and no wonder Fields went to bed with a goat. I remember a line I had with Chico in *Go West*, when they're fleecing me of my last ten bucks. I say, "You love your brother, don't you?" And he says, "No, but I'm used to him." I wrote most of the gags on that picture myself. I sent the writers out to write job applications. There was a writer on that show called J. Slavens McNutt. You have to give up after that.

In The Big Store, *however, you finally got around to playing Wolf J. Flywheel from your old radio show.*

That picture was about as funny as the Jap attack on Pearl Harbor. It was our last fling with Maggie Dumont. At the end of that movie the finance company hauls us off in my old broken-down car, the three of us with Maggie, dragging us out under

the end credits because we hadn't paid twelve years'
installments. That was just what life was for us at
that time.

There were two more Marx Brothers movies, A Night
in Casablanca *and* Love Happy. *And you made three
movies solo.*

Boy, was I solo. I used to sit alone in the balcony of
the Marquis Theater, smoking or sleeping. There
were no girls there to chat up. The manager's wife
came in and sat in the box office, trying to sell
tickets. Luckily, they didn't show any of our pictures,
or maybe I just fell asleep.

Was it about that time you got an offer from radio?

That was with Pabst Blue Ribbon Beer. A sickly brew,

but it sure saved my bacon. Gummo got that for me. A half-hour show for CBS. They gave me $2,500 a week. Yippee! That shook me out of the doldrums. We had great stars on the show. Lucille Ball, Joan Bennett, Charles Laughton. He loved it. He didn't even have to dress up as the Hunchback of Notre Dame. You can come as you are on radio. I just wore my pajamas and an old dickey I found in grandpa's shoebox.

Still, you also made A Night in Casablanca.

Chico was in trouble again, and United Artists put up the moolah. Warner Brothers tried to stop us. They had made *Casablanca* with Humphrey Bogart and they claimed they owned the rights in the title. I wrote them that I had no idea that Warner Brothers owned the city of Casablanca. Maybe their great-grandfather, Ferdinand Balboa Warner, discovered it on his way to Burbank. They wrote another coupla times, and then gave up. By the time we made the movie, the war was over. At the preview I knew we had a stinker. We'd shot some good scenes but the director cut them up and ruined the picture. He couldn't direct his way out of a spitoon. At least it was better than *The Big Store*, which isn't saying a whole lot.

There were some good scenes, with Sig Rumann as a Nazi spy, chasing Harpo around the room. Some nice stuff in the Hotel Casablanca you were running, and with Chico in the Camel Cab company. Lisette Verea was the female foil in that movie instead of Maggie Dumont.

She was so slinky none of us could get our hands on her, not even Harpo. I have a line where I look at her waggling her ass and I say, "That reminds me, I have to get my watch fixed." Nobody understood that, but it sounded good. Harpo was getting a bit old for chasing dames. He'd settled down, and adopted four kids. He said he had four windows in his house and he wanted to see a baby in each window when he came back from work. So did I, but not that kind of baby. Chico was going around the world playing the piano, going back to his original stage act. I was married again by then, and moved into Sunset Plaza Drive with Kay and Melinda. So I was snug as a bug.

But in 1947 you were starring, as the only Marx in the movie, in Copacabana, *with Carmen Miranda.*

She had bananas on her head and bats in her belfry. She was from Brazil, you know, and I couldn't make out a word she was saying. We got along just fine. Then I made *Double Dynamite* with Frank Sinatra and Jane Russell and *A Girl in Every Port* with William Bendix. Jane Russell had melons that could feed the starving masses in China, and Bendix bulged in all the wrong places. He was a sweet man, though. Sinatra was a skinny little thing. Can you imagine that he got so big? Sheer showmanship. I had a good line in *A Girl in Every Port*. I tell a waiter to pay the fare of a taxi I've just arrived in and he says, "To whom should I charge it?" And I say, "To experience!" Well, it was the best we could do. I was getting fed up with the sheer grind of the movies. Getting up at six in the morning to be dragged to the studio where a bald makeup man with halitosis slaps Max Factor pancake on your puss. I was sure of one thing: I never wanted to make another Marx Brothers movie in my life.

And then you made Love Happy.

The gods looked down, and laughed. But not at
the jokes. Boy, were they lousy. Harpo was getting
restless and wanted to get back into pictures. Chico
needed a job, so he got roped in. United Artists gave
us a producer called Lester Cowan. He'd done *My
Little Chickadee* with Bill Fields and Mae West and
they both hated his guts. He made Harpo so mad he
even spat on him on the set. They begged me to be
the stuffing in this turkey so I played Sam Grunion,
private detective. I'd been tracking the Romanoff
diamonds, or something dumb like that, for years,
"Through the Khyber Pass, over the Pyrenees and
into Gimbel's basement" … where I should've stayed
put. I had on this Sherlock Holmes outfit and prayed
that nobody would recognize me. That was absolutely
the end. Chico and Harpo went off to London after

the shoot to play the Palladium. I should've gone to Rio de Janeiro with La Miranda! But instead I got a new job on radio with John Guedel. He had a show called *People Are Funny*, with Art Linkletter as the MC.

And that became You Bet Your Life.

Praise the Lord! Say, do you think we can get another cup of coffee? I think I just dozed off. Have you said anything worth hearing in the last hour and a half?

Not really.

Well, that's why I didn't hear it.

Well, that's why I didn't say it.

Hey, who's writing this stuff, me or you?

TELEVISION AND THE "SECRET WORD"

In the 1950s Groucho learned to adapt to a
new medium, television, with the quiz show,
You Bet Your Life. Television imposed a whole
new set of rules for the working comedian.
Groucho was now not just a movie and stage
star but a familiar figure who entered people's
homes. Instead of lines and gags written
by professionals, he had to contend with
spontaneous dialogue from ordinary people
chosen to appear on the show. A new Groucho
emerged—one who had some relationship
with the old curmudgeon of wisecracks, but
who also found a completely new voice.

You Bet Your Life began on radio in 1947 and then ran on television for more than eleven years. What was your impression of TV in the early years?

I found TV very educational. Every time somebody switched it on, I went into another room and read a book. In the beginning, you know, not a lot of people had TV sets. They didn't fit with the furniture, and had these kind of bulbous screens. You had to stand in the corner with the aerial and then bang it with a brush or a hammer every time the picture broke up. Now nobody can live without it. But our show was much better on television because people could see the contestants. They were just ordinary Joes and Janes from all over the country and they were much more entertaining than I was. In fact I was about as much use as the prop they displayed in the show when a contestant hit on the "Secret Word," which triggered big cash prizes. It was a wooden duck with my mustache on. At least I didn't need to paint mine on every day. I'd got bored with that so I grew my own. And here it is *(fingering his mustache)*. A pathetic thing but I'm used to it. I thought of growing a beard to catch spaghetti but my kids wouldn't let me.

Television, though, got you a whole new audience. People who were too young to have seen the old Marx Brothers movies rediscovered Groucho Marx. And later the movies themselves were shown on TV.

That's true. People could watch the way we were in the old days and compare it with the corpse they saw on TV. I had a perfect straight man, George Fenneman. He was a great guy. Of course, we also had writers. People thought it was all off the cuff but there were writers on that show. They had to keep it loose so that I could be as free as possible with the contestants. I only went on the show because I heard they were giving away a thousand dollars, and then I found out I was the one giving it away. It was a new kind of thing, at that time. Now everybody knows about quiz shows.

Your humor had to be different on that show, didn't it? There was stuff you couldn't get away with.

Absolutely. The funniest part of the show was when I'm chatting with the guests between the questions. One lady said she had ten kids and her husband had a job with a 24-hour call-out. But he got home between calls. So I said, "Imagine if he had a job around the house." They cut that out. The show was never live, it was always edited. Another lady was bragging about having eight kids and how she enjoyed it, and I said, "I like my cigar, but I take it out of my mouth once in a while." They seemed to miss that. But it was a lot of fun. Most of the jokes were clean. One guy was a tree surgeon, so I asked him, "Did you ever fall out of a patient?" Some people said that I insulted the guests. But I got no complaints at the time. They all expected it. It got so that if I passed somebody in the street and didn't insult them, they were really mad at me. That got awfully tiresome after a while. Then I noticed the guests on the show were getting funnier than I was. That was a good time to quit.

The last show was in 1961.

People got bored with it and I'd been dead for five years. But I did some more television after that, with NBC. Chico tried to do a TV show, some years before.

He played an ice cream man called Papa Romani. The show aired for a while, but it didn't go anywhere. Harpo tried, but he could hardly do the talk shows. In the end he wrote his book, *Harpo Speaks*. And I'd done my own book, *Groucho and Me*. That was a lot of fun. By that time, I'd been divorced and married again. My third wife, Eden, was a model. We stayed home a lot and I read more books. She used to paint. We moved to a bigger house. I liked to fix the plumbing. By the time I fixed it, the whole of Beverly Hills was flooded.

Harpo and Gummo moved out to Palm Springs. Zeppo moved there, too. They wanted me to join them, so I bought a second house there. But the desert wasn't for me. Gummo retired from the agenting business and did nothing for 25 years but look at the mountains and play golf. Can you beat that? If I did nothing, it would kill me.

The three Marx Brothers last appeared together in a CBS show called The Incredible Jewel Robbery, *in 1959. It lasted 30 minutes. Do you remember it? It was hosted by Ronald Reagan and your last words on the show were, "We aren't talking till we see our lawyer."*

Which is the advice I should have taken on this interview. I'm going to see my attorney as soon as he finishes law school. They tell me Ronald Reagan went on to be President, so at least somebody made it after that turkey. But I thought we were going to talk about the good old days. I did enjoy *You Bet Your Life*. It put me in touch with America, with people of all shapes and sizes. Tall people, fat people, broad people, thin people, midgets. There was a Mexican dancer, called Ramiro Gonzalez Gonzalez. I said we should start an act called "The Two Hot Tamales," and he said to me, no, it should be "Gonzalez Gonzalez and Marx." So I said to him, "Great billing. Two people in the act and I get third place." It was good fun. And I learned all kinds of big words and crazy facts. Do you know what sort of animal is a dromedary? Do you know who was our only bachelor President? Do you know who wrote "The Ballad of Barbara Fritchie?" Who was Popeye's sweetheart? What kind of sauce is served on Eggs Benedict? What do you do in bed when you get home at night, you beast? Oh, the shame of it all!

Hey, do you want to know today's Secret Word? It's "Scram!" There's one person too many in this room and I think it's you.

I'd like to talk about your writing.

Why didn't you say so in the first place? The nerve of some people! I ought to join a club and beat you over the head with it. Well, just tell me what you want to know and I'll see to it that you never work in this business again. And remember to get Essolube, that hydrorefined motor oil. It's regular priced, so it's cheaper than salad oil and gives you the cramps twice as fast! Oops! Wrong show. Well, get on with it! I can't hang around all day.

THE SUMMING UP, OR LIFE LESSONS OF AN OLD HAM

Give or take a year or two, Groucho Marx
entertained audiences for three-quarters of
a century. But he often said that his real love
was writing, the solitary pleasure of expressing
his thoughts on the page. He was also a keen
reader. At the time that he flourished as a
performer, American popular culture was
entering the mainstream and a new critical
voice was questioning the American Dream.
Satirical writers such as James Thurber and
H.L. Mencken informed Groucho's thinking
away from stage and screen. His own work as
a comedian reflected their influence and left
lessons for others following him to learn.

You always said what you most enjoyed was your writing. Can you sum up, after your long experience in performing—life on the stage, vaudeville, Broadway, the movies—what it is that makes Groucho Marx tick?

It's my watch, kid. And come to think of it, didn't those men in white coats say they were coming about now to take you back to the asylum? In my time, people like you had a cap and bell so decent folk could move aside on the sidewalk. Why don't I bore a hole in you and let the sap run out?

During your career, you published four books, worked with other writers on several compilations, had one book of your letters published, and you also wrote many short articles and essays for The New Yorker, *the* New York Times, *the* Saturday Evening Post, *the* Hollywood Reporter, Readers' Digest, *and all sorts of other newspapers and magazines. All that was from the 1920s, wasn't it?*

Well, *The New Yorker* was started up by Harold Ross, who was a complete fruitcake. But he had some great writers, like James Thurber, Robert Benchley, Dorothy Parker. They were mostly the same people who used to meet in the Algonquin with Harpo. They loved Harpo because they could say the smartest things and he only cared about playing cards. Thurber was writing stuff that was really funny and smart at the same time, and he also drew those incredible cartoons. He published *Is Sex Necessary?*, which was a fantastic bestseller. Up to then I'd just scribbled my own lines in our sketches and acts. But then I got the bug. Kaufman and Alex Woollcott got me some pieces published in the *New York Times*. Then I published *Beds*, in 1930, which was about people, not what they got up to in them. But it was pretty much of a flop. People refused to have anything to do with *Beds* for years. Entire families slept standing up.

Apart from Thurber, which writers really influenced you at the time?

Mostly H.L. Mencken. He wrote about all the things that needed shaking up in the country. He attacked all the idiots who were leading us to the Wall Street Crash, the "boobocracy." He didn't write what people wanted to hear. He was ready to be unpopular. He wrote that the people who were most admired in the country were liars, and those they hated the most were the people who dared tell the truth.

And wasn't that your character, the "Grouch," the guy

that told the most outrageous lies to show up all the hypocrites and social climbers? Like the art critic Roscoe W. Chandler in Animal Crackers, *who's actually Abie the Fishmonger from Czechoslovakia?*

That was George Kaufman's material. I learned a lot from him, too. But I thought I'd stick to short pieces, rather than novels or plays. People expected me to make 'em laugh, not to make 'em think. That was Mencken's job. I was just a working ham actor. He was brought up with Mark Twain and Tolstoy and Shakespeare. I was brought up with Swayne's Rats and Cats.

Before that, when you were in Chicago, there was a bookstore you used to go to, wasn't there? Where you could meet writers like Carl Sandburg or Theodore Dreiser. There's an archive script from that period

*which may be the first thing you wrote, called "Art
in Vaudeville." That was in 1919, I believe. There's a
Madame Vici in that sketch who says, "I'll never forget
how the Greeks fell at my feet," and your character says,
"I had a couple of them at my feet this morning, but
fifteen cents is too much for a shine." And that was years
before you met Margaret Dumont.*

With a memory like yours, my friend, you should
be in the Smithsonian. In a glass case. But those
were just gags. You could find those in all the joke
books. When you're writing for readers, you can't
rely on one-liners. Kaufman certainly taught me
that. And Bob Benchley. Thurber was great at that.
He never wrote gags, but he made pictures for you
in words that you could never get out of your mind.
Like *The Day the Dam Broke*. You were caught up in
his crazy world.

Which is a good description of a Marx Brothers movie.

Well, we didn't see it like that. It was just a job. When you're on the set, you have to keep out of the way of all the cables and make sure you're in shot at the right time if you don't want to be delivering your lines just to a sweaty Polish grip with hair popping out of his vest chewing a stick of gum. Of course, the audience thinks you're making it up as you go along and having a good time. But that's the director's job, and the editor's, to make it seem so. The only guy who knew exactly what he wanted on the set was Chaplin. He could be either side of the camera and still be in total control. When we first met him in vaudeville he looked like a starving clergyman whose collar was on the wrong way. He said he was being offered 60 dollars a week with Mack Sennett and asked me if I thought it was worth it. I told him anything was better than sitting in a stinking dressing room with a performing mule farting in your face.

Did you admire his work?

He was a great silent talent. But he knew he couldn't talk worth a damn. In the end he only talked in the movies because he felt he had to speak out against fascism. I admire him for that.

And the other comedians?

We all liked Buster Keaton, and Harold Lloyd. There were stables of comedians in those days, whipped to work by Mack Sennett and Hal Roach. It was like working in a factory. We decided right at the start that we'd be our own men. Chico thought of that first. He organized us into our different characters.

He was a very organized guy, under all that Italian nonsense. He negotiated our contracts on Broadway and at Paramount. But he could never keep hold of his own money. It drove us all crazy. I could look after myself, and Harpo was smart, too. Zeppo got fed up with being the kid brother and became an agent like Gummo. Chico was the one most like our mother. She loved organizing, too. She had all sorts of acts in Chicago, not just the Marx Brothers. She had a training school for young actresses in our house, teaching them to dance and sing. It was like paradise for Chico and Harpo. They went haring up and down the staircases, chasing them. It sure taught those poor little gals to be nimble. Yes sir, you had to get up early if you wanted to get out of bed in our house. If you wanted to get *into* bed, you just had to stick around. I guess we were pretty wild. Once in Mobile the local Rabbi liked our show so much he invited us to Friday night supper, before the Sabbath. Then on Thursday night he went into his daughter's room and found Chico and Harpo there. They jumped out the window, but Chico turned back on the window sill and asked, "Is Friday night still okay?"

So, in a way, on stage and screen you were just being yourselves?

You're coming back to documentary again. But in vaudeville it was always the audience that had the final say. When we were doing our tour before *A Day at the Races*, we'd keep changing the scene after every performance. Sometimes it would come down to one word. I had a line that went "That's the most— whatever—proposal I've ever heard!" We tried every possible word in there—disgusting, revolting, obnoxious, repulsive, and so on. But the word that got the biggest laugh was "nauseating." Now don't ask me why. Even Henry James couldn't have explained it. So if the audience liked us in movies it was because we'd tested as much as we could, years before, on the stage. In Nacogdoches in Texas, about 100 years ago, we were so unfunny the audience beat it out of the theater to see a runaway mule. That's when we understood that you have to work like a navvy to get 'em on your side. Because if they won't pay to see your act, you don't eat. It's simple as that. Everything else is horse feathers.

Have you any advice for any young people wanting to get into show business?

Don't grow old. Growing old is easy, you just have to live long enough. Take good care of your teeth—you don't want to end up eating steak tartare with your gums. If you've got brothers or sisters, take the bed nearest the toilet. A tax inspector in the bush is worth two in the house. The more money you earn in this racket, the quicker you go to a higher bracket. Don't do anything for posterity, because posterity will do nothing for you. The secret of life is honesty and fair dealing—if you can fake that, you've got it made. And don't forget: art is art and east is east and west is west and if you take cranberries and stew them like applesauce they taste much more like prunes than rhubarb does.

Groucho Marx, thank you very much.

No, no, I'm not getting into that routine again. Well, I've had a perfectly wonderful afternoon, but this wasn't it. *(To the waitress)* "Honey, can you bring us the check?" I'll tell you just one more thing. All of show business is made of two kinds of material. In the old days, an old timer would come to the theater box office and wouldn't even bother to look at the billing. He'd ask just one question about the program: Is it sad or high-kicking? That's all you need to know. *(The waitress brings Groucho the bill—he glances at it and hands it to me)* Twenty-four dollars and 65 cents! It's an outrage! If I were you, I wouldn't pay it.

DOUBLE-TAKE. MUSIC UP.
ALL PEEK INTO CAMERA AND FREEZE.
WAITRESS HOLDS UP GIANT MATSOH-BALL.
RAPID FADE.

REFILL?

Coffee with Groucho is a fictional conversation. Selected quips are quoted from Marx Brothers movies: *The Cocoanuts*, *Animal Crackers*, *Monkey Business*, *Horse Feathers*, *Duck Soup*, *A Night at the Opera*, *A Day at the Races*, *Go West*, *The Big Store*, *A Night in Casablanca*, *Love Happy*. Assorted Groucho Marx sayings, both authentic and apocryphal, are sprinkled throughout.

SELECTED BIBLIOGRAPHY OF BOOKS ON GROUCHO AND THE MARX BROTHERS

Joe Adamson, *Groucho, Harpo, Chico and Sometimes Zeppo* (New York: Simon & Schuster, 1973)

Richard J. Anobile, *The Marx Brothers Scrapbook* (New York: Darien House, 1973)

Hector Arce, *Groucho* (New York: G.P. Putnam & Sons, 1979)

Hector Arce & Groucho Marx, *The Groucho Phile* (New York: Galahad Books 1976)

Robert Bader (ed.), *Groucho Marx & other Short Stories and Tall Tales* (London: Faber & Faber, 1993)

Michael Barson (ed.), *Flywheel, Shyster, & Flywheel, the Marx Brothers' Lost Radio Shows* (New York: Pantheon Books, 1988)

Kyle Crichton, *The Marx Brothers* (New York: Doubleday & Co., 1950)

Stefan Kanfer, *The Essential Groucho, Writings by, for, and about Groucho Marx* (New York: Vintage, 2000)

Stefan Kanfer, *Groucho, the Life and Times of Julius Henry Marx* (New York: Knopf, 2000)

Simon Louvish, *Monkey Business, the Lives and Legends of the Marx Brothers* (London: Faber & Faber, 1999; New York: St. Martin's Press, 2000)

Arthur Marx, *Life with Groucho* (New York: Simon & Schuster, 1954)

Groucho Marx, *Beds* (New York: Farrar & Reinhart, 1930)

Groucho Marx, *Many Happy Returns* (New York: Simon & Schuster, 1942)

Groucho Marx, *Groucho and Me* (New York: Bernard Geis Associates, 1959)

Groucho Marx, *Memoirs of a Mangy Lover* (New York: Bernard Geis Associates, 1963)

Groucho Marx, *The Groucho Letters* (New York: Simon & Schuster, 1967)

Harpo Marx (with Rowland Barber), *Harpo Speaks* (New York: Random House, 1961)

Maxine Marx, *Growing Up With Chico* (Prentice Hall, 1980)

Miriam Marx, *Love, Groucho* (London, Faber & Faber, 1992)

Glenn Mitchell, *The Marx Brothers Encyclopedia* (London: B.T. Batsford, 1996)

MAJOR WEBSITES

www.grouchoworld.com

www.marx-brothers.org

THE MOVIES OF THE MARX BROTHERS

The Cocoanuts, 1929

This comedy-musical adapted from the stage features Groucho as a Florida hotel owner faced with a series of exasperating and farcical mishaps. Notable for its live score and its dance numbers, the movie also features the famous "viaduct/why a duck?" gag.

Animal Crackers, 1930

Groucho, as celebrated explorer Captain Spaulding, attends a party thrown for him by Lillian Roth's society hostess. Chaos ensues as the Marx Brothers investigate the theft of a valuable painting.

Monkey Business, 1931

The brothers play stowaways on a ship crossing the Atlantic from Europe to America. The movie features Maurice Chevalier impressions by the brothers at passport control and the only known movie recording of Harpo's voice.

Horse Feathers, 1932
Speakeasies and prohibition jokes add a topical edge to this campus-based comedy, in which the brothers turn their attention to the farcical politics of college football teams. The movie features the song "Everyone Says I Love You."

Duck Soup, 1933
"Take two turkeys, one goose, four cabbages, but no duck, and mix them together. After one taste, you'll duck soup for the rest of your life." So went Groucho's explanation for the movie's title, which has little to do with the imaginary country of Freedonia in which *Duck Soup* is set.

A Night at the Opera, 1935
Marking the inception of an era of "softer" Marx Brothers movies, with Groucho's acerbic wit toned down at the request of producer Irving Thalberg, *A Night at the Opera* sees the brothers bring romantic and operatic success to a pair of young lovers.

A Day at the Races, 1937
The brothers take up gambling at the racetrack in order to save the fate of the sanitarium at which Groucho, although only qualified as a veterinarian, works as a doctor. *A Day at the Races* was the biggest Marx Brothers box-office success.

Room Service, 1938
The brothers play down-and-out theater producers attempting to avoid being evicted from their hotel room in this relatively poorly received farce, adapted from a Broadway play.

At the Circus, 1939
Harpo, Chico, and Groucho play Punchy the strongman's assistant, Antonio the circus hand, and Loophole the lawyer, as they attempt to save their circus from bankruptcy.

Go West, 1940
Groucho tries to extort money for a ticket to the Wild West from Harpo and Chico, but is himself conned

out of the deeds to a gold mine. Together the brothers embark upon a race to claim back the deeds—providing a spectacular locomotive scene along the way.

The Big Store, 1941
The brothers take over a failing department store, attempting to pass themselves off as salesmen and introducing the salespitch "Where everything is a good buy, Goodbye!"

A Night in Casablanca, 1946
In this loose parody of the classic movie *Casablanca*, Groucho takes over a Casablanca hotel following the murders of its previous managers. Aided by his brothers, he discovers Nazi loot hidden in the hotel, which soon leads to much intrigue as the Nazis attempt to recover their booty.

Love Happy, 1950
Skilled shoplifter Harpo lands the brothers in hot water as he unwittingly includes a sardine can holding the Romanoff diamonds in the consignment of food he steals for a group of impoverished young dramatists on Broadway. Cue a manic escape from the jewel thieves who had secreted the diamonds in the can. The movie features a brief performance from a young Marilyn Monroe.

MOVIES STARRING GROUCHO
Copacabana, 1947
Double Dynamite, 1951
A Girl in Every Port, 1952

MOVIES FEATURING GROUCHO IN MINOR ROLES
Mr. Music, 1950
Will Success Spoil Rock Hunter?, 1957
The Story of Mankind, 1957
Skidoo, 1968

INDEX